Ellen James

Lisa

Harlequin Books

TORONTO • NEW YORK • LONDON
AMSTERDAM • PARIS • SYDNEY • HAMBURG
STOCKHOLM • ATHENS • TOKYO • MILAN
MADRID • WARSAW • BUDAPEST • AUCKLAND

ISBN 0-373-70738-X

LISA

Copyright © 1997 by Ellen James.

This edition published by arrangement with Harlequin Books S.A.

® and TM are trademarks of the publisher. Trademarks indicated with
® are registered in the United States Patent and Trademark Office, the
Canadian Trade Marks Office and in other countries.

Printed in U.S.A.

PROLOGUE

BARE WALLS, empty rooms. No memories here.

Helene walked through the small apartment. *Her* apartment, she reminded herself. Over seventy years old, and she would be living on her own for the very first time. She didn't know whether to laugh or cry at the thought.

The telephone rang, startling her. It had been hooked up only this morning; who could be calling? She stared at the phone, letting it ring several more times. Obviously it was someone stubborn. She walked over and picked up the receiver.

"Hello?" she said, disliking the tentative way she spoke. A woman on her own should be forceful, decisive.

"Hello," came the gruff voice of her husband.

"Merrick...how did you get this number?" Now she sounded cranky, and she hadn't intended that, either.

"Amy," Merrick said, terse as ever.

Helene frowned. She'd made her daughter swear not to give him the number. But Amy was good-hearted and impulsive, and seemed determined to get her parents back together again. What a supreme irony. Helene did laugh, bleakly.

"Want to share the joke?" Merrick asked.

Helene couldn't say anything. Certainly she couldn't expose her misery and self-doubt to him. But all this trouble had started out with the best of intentions, hadn't it? Helene had been worried about the years of estrangement between her three daughters—Amy, Lisa and Megan—and a few months ago she'd concocted what seemed the perfect plan. She and Merrick would feign marital difficulties, and surely that would give the Hardaway girls a reason to unite—a joint purpose in setting their parents straight. But somehow, the plan had succeeded too well. All too soon, the feigned problems in their marriage had become painfully real.

"Helene," Merrick said.

She gripped the receiver. "Yes...I'm still here. Why did you call?"

"I need a reason to call my own wife?"

"Merrick," she said on a warning note. She heard his stifled curse on the other end of the line, and then he began again.

"I thought you should know that Lisa decided to take a later flight. She won't arrive until after six tonight."

"You'll pick her up at the airport?"

"Amy wants to. Something about needing a sisterly chat."

Oh, yes, the plan to unite their daughters had worked well enough. Since the whole thing began, this was already the second time Lisa—the youngest—had flown in from Connecticut. The oldest, Megan, too, would arrive from Nebraska next week, and had arranged to stay at Amy's beach house. Megan, Amy, Lisa…the three Hardaway girls, together again in Hurricane Beach.

"At least our daughters are spending more time together," Helene murmured, almost to herself. "We've accomplished that much."

Merrick gave another grumbled curse. "Turns out the three of them have some crazy idea about planning an anniversary party for us."

"What on earth makes you think that—"

"I'm good at picking up clues," Merrick said. "And our daughter Amy is not exactly close-mouthed. Apparently, this anniversary bash is supposed to convince us we shouldn't throw fifty years out the window. But I'm not the one who needs convincing—am I, Helene?"

If only she could make him understand! Pretending that their marriage was in trouble had stirred up so much unexpected resentment and bitterness in her. So many stifled dreams had begun to haunt her. Finally, Helene had confronted the truth: she'd spent years loving Merrick, but years also bending to him, molding herself to whatever he needed and desired. And she'd known, with terrible clarity, that she could no longer go on bending. Despite her fears for the future, she had recognized one irrevocable fact: she could not be the woman her husband wanted her to be.

"Helene," Merrick said. "We have to talk sooner or later. About whether or not we're going to sell the property, for one thing."

It had become very much a sore spot between

herself and Merrick—this decision about whether or not to sell their beachfront property to Silver Sands Development. "I know what you're really thinking," Helene said quietly. "You're thinking that all you have to do is convince me to come over to your side. You want me to agree to the sale…just as I've always agreed to everything. And then, as far as you're concerned, all our problems will be over."

"I thought you were happy with me. I thought you had everything you wanted—"

"This is what I need now, Merrick. A place of my own. Decisions of my own." She was proud of herself for speaking firmly at last. In spite of the pain, the sudden loneliness, she needed to be away from him. For years and years she had loved Merrick Hardaway with all her heart…but she could no longer be with him.

All the pretending was over.

CHAPTER ONE

IT WAS HIM. Blue-gray eyes, dark hair swept back carelessly from his forehead, as if the gulf breeze had had its way with him. Just as he'd had his way with Lisa, some fifteen years ago. Yes...it was Matt Connell, all right.

Lisa ducked behind the magazine rack at Thompson's Drugstore. She felt an odd, constricted feeling inside, and she had to force herself to take a steadying breath. This was absurd, she told herself. She was no longer an insecure, awestruck sixteen-year-old. She was over thirty. A woman with her own life now, her own career. Her own man. She tried to conjure up a reassuring image of Patrick. Handsome, good-natured Patrick, waiting for her back at the bed-and-breakfast. But somehow the image faded. And all Lisa could remember was a shimmering summer day all those years go, when she'd first looked into Matt Connell's blue-gray eyes, and known she would do anything to keep on looking.

Now, with an effort, Lisa reached out and picked up a magazine at random. She flipped through the pages automatically, pretending to be engrossed. She was hiding out in her hometown drugstore—

and meanwhile, the very first love of her life, Matt
Connell, was one aisle over. Suddenly she was
tempted to make her getaway straight out the door.
Or she could stay here behind the magazines until
she was absolutely certain that Matt had left the
place. In other words, she could go on hiding.

She turned and gazed out the window. The view
was something that had often haunted her dreams:
the boardwalk stretching all along the curve of the
beach, the sands sparkling silver-white in the sun,
the blue-green of the gulf waters, the old-fashioned
cupola of the marina clubhouse rising on the ho-
rizon. And the wharf beyond…unseen from this
vantage, but Lisa knew it well. That was where
Matt had first kissed her, one magical summer's
night.

She grabbed another magazine and headed down
the aisle. She'd get what she had come for. She'd
go about her business like a normal, rational adult,
and she would forget Matt Connell. After all, she'd
managed to forget him once before. She refused to
look around as she went along, refused the possibility that she might catch a glimpse of him again.
She found a certain row of medicines, and surveyed
the choices available. Usually, she didn't have any
trouble making up her mind about things, but even
this minor decision seemed too complex at the moment. She read one label, then another, but not a
single word seemed to make sense. She could feel
Matt's presence in this small store, even if she
couldn't see him. It was almost as if the humid

summer air had bestirred itself, and now vibrated a warning to her.

"Ridiculous," she muttered. She grabbed something in a box, hardly noticing what it was, then she set off down another aisle. And there he was, standing in profile before her. Matt Connell, his features etched in the uncompromising lines she had once known so well. *Uncompromising*...that had been the best word to describe him back then. Lisa was the one who had yielded, who had given far too much of herself.

Matt was no longer an eighteen-year-old boy, of course. He was a man. He had worn well with the passage of time, but he *had* worn. Subtle grooves had worked their way into his forehead, as if he'd grown accustomed to frowning. His hair was still dark and luxuriant, still curling a bit long over his collar, but the way it swept back from his face was different, giving him a new sternness. There was something rigid and aloof in the way he stood, apparently absorbed in his own thoughts. Obviously he hadn't noticed Lisa yet. She had another chance to escape. She could just back away a few steps, turn and leave. This chance encounter at the drugstore wouldn't have to be an encounter at all.

Lisa actually did take a step backward. It was then Matt glanced up and saw her. He drew his eyebrows together as he studied her, looking faintly puzzled. And, with an unpleasant jolt, Lisa realized he didn't recognize her. Matt Connell, the person who'd once had the power to tear her life apart, didn't even know who she was.

She could still turn away. She could pretend she didn't know *him*. But some reckless pride prevented her from doing that. Instead, she moved a step toward him.

"Hello, Matt," she said coolly.

The look of puzzlement didn't leave his eyes, but it mixed with what seemed a flicker of irritation. She sensed that he preferred to be left alone, and that made her more determined to stay.

"So," she said in on offhand manner. "You're back in town, too."

He didn't answer. She almost had to admire that he made no pretense at politeness. He didn't try to cover up the fact that he couldn't place her. He just gazed at her with that slight frown, as if waiting for her to go elsewhere.

She wouldn't oblige him. "I didn't know you spent the summers here anymore," she said.

"I don't." He spoke even these few words grudgingly. But she could tell that his voice had deepened, grown richer.

"I moved away a long time ago," she said, and wondered why she'd offered the information. He was making it clear that he didn't want a friendly chat.

He hadn't been like this once. Those many years ago, he'd been fully aware of his own charm, his own ability to entice. And he had used that ability to devastating effect. But the Matt Connell before her now seemed to have lost all tolerance for charm…his own or anyone else's.

What was making her linger here? Already he'd

gone back to perusing the shelves of candy before him: gumdrops, licorice, chocolates, caramels. From the look of him now, Matt hardly seemed the type for anything sweet.

"Saltwater taffy," she said, the words slipping out before she could stop them. Matt gave her only a brief glance, not even bothering to ask what she meant. His very disinterest compelled her to say more.

"You used to like saltwater taffy," she said, managing to keep her tone offhand. "The stuff you could buy out on Conway's Pier. But they probably don't sell it anymore."

"I wouldn't know." Again he spoke reluctantly. He leaned down and picked up a bag of butterscotch candy, jiggling it a little in his hand. At last he glanced at Lisa again. "They're not for me," he said.

Lisa understood immediately. The butterscotch was intended for some woman or other. Perhaps Matt was going to do flowers and candy—the whole bit. Why should that be a surprise? Even at eighteen, he'd understood the value of romantic gestures. Lisa despised the emotions swirling through her. Anger, and a baffling sense of longing she hadn't experienced in years. But what did it matter to her if Matt Connell was embarking on yet another summer affair?

She turned to go, only to find herself pausing and examining him once more. Admittedly, *this* Matt did not appear the type for countenancing romantic gestures. He stared broodingly at the butterscotches, as if they had offended him in some way.

"It's interesting," Lisa said. "Women still do fall for that kind of thing."

Matt gave her another quizzical glance. And Lisa wondered why she couldn't just leave the drugstore. Why did she have to go on standing here beside him, saying whatever came to mind?

She went on in spite of herself. "It's true," she said. "Women, for some silly reason, still go for all the trappings. Valentines, red roses...even butterscotch."

He seemed to consider this. "So," he said, hefting the bag of candy from one hand to the other. "You think these will do the trick?"

"Absolutely. She'll fall for it." Lisa heard the acid sound of her own voice, and realized she had to stop this conversation. "Well, goodbye—"

"I take it you don't fall for anything." Again he spoke as if each word came reluctantly, as if he'd lost all inclination for small talk.

Lisa hesitated. "I've learned," she said at last. "I'm not as foolish as I used to be."

When he gazed at her this time, his look was enigmatic. Blue smoke, that was the color of his eyes. Lisa told herself to glance away, but she couldn't. She just gazed back at Matt, feeling that odd tightening inside. And suddenly she remembered exactly how it felt to be sixteen, aching for something you couldn't even describe, yearning naively for all your unspoken wishes to come true.

Somehow, she finally did glance away, focusing

her gaze on the magazines and the small box of medicine she clutched. Matt looked at the box, too.

"It's not for me," she said ironically. "It's for— a friend. Someone with…indigestion." How mundane that sounded, how staid. Lisa tried to remind herself that there wasn't anything staid about Patrick Dannon, and anyone could get a touch of indigestion.

Once again Matt seemed to give her words grave consideration. "Hope he feels better."

Lisa felt herself flushing. It hadn't been her intention to inform Matt that she had a man in her life. That wasn't necessary. She could very well stand here on her own, and prove to him that she'd gone on, that what had happened fifteen years ago hadn't defeated her.

It seemed that, just now, she'd forgotten two rather important details. Number one, Matt didn't know the whole, painful truth of that long-ago summer. Number two, he no longer even remembered her name.

She gave him a smile she knew was tinged with bitterness. That much she couldn't help.

"Nice talking to you," she said, proud of the negligent tone in her voice. "Hope the butterscotch does its job." When she turned this time, she really did walk away. She was almost at the end of the aisle when he spoke, his own voice quiet.

"Goodbye, Lisa Hardaway."

AMY WAS AT IT AGAIN—taking charge, behaving optimistically, as if all she had to do was whip up a family meal, and all problems in the Hardaway clan would be resolved. With a familiar mixture of exasperation and defensiveness, Lisa sat on a stool at the kitchen counter and watched her older sister move around. Amy washed lettuce in the quick, competent way she had, then began chopping celery. She smiled to herself as she worked. That was another thing about Amy—she seemed remarkably happy these days. And why not? She was engaged to be married. Her fiancé, in fact, was none other than Jon Costas…Lisa's very own ex-husband.

Lisa winced, just thinking about it. Her gaze strayed across the kitchen and into the living room, where a small group had gathered: Lisa's mother, Helene, Lisa's current boyfriend, Patrick, and Lisa's *former* husband, Jon. What a combination. From here, Lisa could see Jon as he leaned down to pet Sam, Amy's golden retriever. The dog thumped his tail appreciatively. It appeared that no one in the Hardaway clan had any problem with Jon and Amy's engagement. No one but Lisa.

She told herself that she ought to be glad for her sister. How often did two people find genuine love together? Just because these two people were Lisa's ex-husband and her sister, that was no reason to object—

"Lisa," Amy said, her tone earnest. Apparently, she'd caught the direction of Lisa's gaze. "I wish you would just let me explain, for once."

Lisa sighed. "I understand. The two of you fell in love. End of story."

"No—it's not the end. Not as long as there's any chance I'm hurting my own sister."

"Look, Amy," Lisa said. "You shouldn't pay any attention to what *I* think. If you and Jon are right for each other, you should grab him and forget about everything else."

"I can't forget about family," Amy said stubbornly. "I can never forget about that."

Lisa sighed again, and asked herself why she couldn't just put on a cheery face about Amy and Jon. That way, at least Amy would stop plaguing her with questions.

Here came another question—Lisa saw it forming on her sister's very pretty and very expressive face. "You told me you didn't love Jon anymore," Amy murmured. "That maybe you never truly had loved him. You even have a new man in your life. So what is it, Lisa? Why is it that every time you look at Jon and me, you seem so...so uncomfortable?"

Why, indeed? Lisa glanced across at the living room again. She studied her ex-husband from afar. If anything, Jon had grown more attractive over the years, the premature silver of his hair only emphasizing his strong, clear-cut features. Amazing what love could do for a man, giving him an air of contentment he'd never possessed before. Certainly not when he'd been with Lisa.

Failure. That was what Jon and Amy made Lisa feel—a sense that she had been failing at love for a very long time now. It had no doubt been a mistake to marry Jon in the first place. But the mis-

takes went back even further…to the summer Lisa
was sixteen, when she had looked into the smoky-
blue eyes of a boy named Matt Connell, and known
that nothing about her life would ever be the same
again.

Lisa realized that she was gripping her hands
tightly on top of the kitchen counter, and that her
sister was observing her with concern.

"Leave it, Amy," she said. "For once, just leave
it alone."

Amy started to speak, but then, surprisingly, she
let the subject go. She went to peer into a pot that
simmered on the stove.

"The sauce is almost done," she announced.
"Lisa, find out what everybody wants to drink. I
have sodas in the fridge—lime, cherry, orange—
but don't forget the wine Patrick brought over last
night. A nice man, your Patrick."

Lisa clenched her teeth. She didn't know why it
bothered her so much to hear Patrick referred to as
"hers." He *was* hers, the first steady man in her
life in quite some time. And he was, admittedly, a
good man. Maybe she finally had a chance to be
successful at a relationship. So why did she feel
annoyed?

Despite Amy's instructions, she remained where
she was, perched on her stool by the counter. It
was time to discuss something besides her own
love life. "It's no use," she told her sister. "You
can go through all the motions, gather us around
the table—the works. You can even go on planning

that big anniversary party of yours. But none of it will convince Mom to move back in with Dad.''

Amy paused in the middle of slicing a tomato, and gazed at Lisa. "Lisa, I wish you wouldn't give up on this. I thought we agreed that at least we were going to try—"

"No, Amy. *You* decided you were going to solve all Mom and Dad's problems. The rest of us are just along for the ride."

Amy's knife attacked the tomato with rather more vigor than Lisa thought necessary. "I wish Megan were here," she muttered. "I wish she didn't have to delay her visit till next week. Because *she'll* come round to my side—"

"Don't get your hopes up," Lisa cautioned. "Megan is just as realistic as I am."

Amy ignored this last comment. She began rummaging through one of the kitchen cabinets, turning away from Lisa purposely, it seemed. As always, Lisa was struck by her sister's vibrancy. Amy's long, strawberry-blond hair rippled down her back. She was gracefully tall—had been since junior high—and Lisa had never once known her to slouch. She always moved confidently, with her head up, as if she expected to see something wonderful off in the distance somewhere. And, wherever she went, she seemed to create a stir of color and warmth. Just look at her kitchen, brimming with such cozy disorder. Red and yellow and green peppers spilled across the counter, pans jostled each other for room in the sink and a Chinese hibiscus flowered extravagantly on the windowsill.

The old sensations came over Lisa—wanting to retreat from her sister's all-encompassing vitality, yet secretly admiring it. Lisa stood restlessly. She went to look inside the refrigerator and saw that Amy had indeed stocked lime, cherry and orange sodas. That was Amy, all right, never content with only one choice. She seemed determined to gather the world into her arms, refusing to admit there might be just a few limitations on how much she could hold. Lisa firmly closed the refrigerator door.

"I never should have let you convince me," she told Amy now. "I never should have let you talk me into coming back to Hurricane Beach." The very name of her hometown evoked unease, turmoil.

Amy started chopping the bell peppers. "Maybe, deep down, you're as concerned about Mom and Dad as I am—and that's why you're here. You won't admit it, that's all. Besides, it's not like I drag you here kicking and screaming all the time. Before last spring, you hadn't been back in ages. Doesn't that tell you something?" It told Lisa a great deal.

It told her that she'd made a new life for herself in Connecticut, building a career where she'd found some genuine meaning at last. It was only when she returned to Florida that the old discontents and longings threatened to overwhelm her. But how could she explain any of that to Amy?

"You'd never have come back at all," her sister went on, "if Mom and Dad weren't making these ridiculous noises about a *divorce*—oh, damn." The knife clattered down and Lisa could see blood forming around a small cut on Amy's finger. Amy cranked on the faucet and stuck her hand underneath the stream of water.

Lisa went to her sister and pressed a paper towel over the cut. "It's a miracle you didn't do worse damage, the way you had that knife flying around. Here—hold it like that. The bleeding will stop in a second or two."

Amy gave her a considering glance. "You've developed a very reassuring tone. Are you like this with those teenage girls of yours?"

Lisa gave a small smile, feeling the tug of "her" girls in Connecticut. Young pregnant teenagers— defiant and difficult to the last one. But they were, after all, kids. And that meant occasionally they could surprise you with laughter, no matter how scared and lonely—and, yes, difficult—they might be.

"You know, Lisa," Amy said, "I really think it's great how you founded that home for girls. It's so worthwhile—"

"Oh, I'm a regular model of virtue," Lisa said caustically. No sense in telling Amy what a struggle it was to keep the girls' shelter open. It wasn't intended as a moneymaking endeavor by any means—and that meant Lisa and the partner who'd helped her found the home were constantly scrounging for donations. Lately, finances had become more precarious. Patrick had offered to help, but so far Lisa had turned him down. She didn't like the thought of complicating their relationship with money matters. She knew, of course, that she could go to her father for money, but she'd always hesitated. Whenever her father got a financial foothold in anything, he had a way of taking over. Somehow, Lisa would just have to come up with the solutions on her own.

"It *is* admirable," Amy insisted. "All the good work you're doing—"

"Yes, I'm just a real whiz at saving the world," Lisa remarked.

Amy shook her head. "You always do this. Someone tries to pay you a compliment, and you get sarcastic. Nothing's wrong with just saying thank-you."

"I'll keep that in mind." Lisa knew she was doing it again, heard the bite in her own voice. But she couldn't seem to help herself whenever she was around family.

Amy blotted her finger with the paper towel, then gave Lisa a hard stare. "Doesn't it drive you crazy, too? The way Mom and Dad are acting about each other... Surely you don't want them to divorce any more than *I* do."

The truth was, the whole thing bothered Lisa a great deal. Her parents had been married almost fifty years. That was something solid, something irrevocable...at least, it was supposed to be. Maybe Lisa disliked coming home to Florida, but in a strange way it had always comforted her knowing that her parents were together. Merrick and Helene Hardaway—even their names sounded like a venerable institution. But a few months ago they had

suddenly started arguing with each other. At first
the reasons for their discord had been close and
murky. Then Merrick had shown interest in selling
the Hardaway beachfront property to a developer,
and Helene had balked at the idea. The disagreement had escalated. Helene had moved out of the
family home, and now Merrick scowled when anyone so much as mentioned his wife's name. What
on earth was going on with them? They'd hardly
disagreed about anything before. It was very dis-
turbing, as if a foundation Lisa had trusted all her
life was slipping beneath her feet.

She didn't know how to share any of this with
her sister. So she merely sat down on one of the
kitchen stools again, propping her elbows on the
counter.

"Mom and Dad are kicking up their heels a little," she said flippantly. "Why not let them—
what's all the fuss?"

Amy muttered something that Lisa couldn't
quite catch.

"You know what?" Amy said, louder now. "*I'll*
go ask everybody what they want to drink." She
went toward the kitchen door, wrapping the paper
towel around her finger. But then she paused and
glanced back at Lisa. "It wouldn't kill you. Now
and then you could actually admit you have feel-
ings. Would it really be so difficult?" With that,
Amy vanished into the living room.

Lisa wearily rubbed her temples. Whether she
was talking to Amy on the phone, or discussing
something face-to-face, she invariably ended up at

odds with her sister. It seemed to be a special talent she had. And like everything else regarding her family, Lisa had no idea what to do about it.

She sat and listened to the simmering of the spaghetti sauce on the stove. Left to herself at last, the thoughts she'd tried to submerge popped up again. Matt Connell... It turned out he *had* recognized her. Oddly enough, the knowledge gave her no satisfaction. All she could do was wonder who would be the lucky recipient of those butterscotch candies.

A woman...was that why he'd come back to Hurricane Beach? But the way Lisa had understood it all those years ago, Matt had known few people in town. He'd come from New Mexico to spend summers in Hurricane Beach with his grandparents, but he'd always been vague about even that much. Lisa had known so little of his personal life, which had made him seem all the more exciting and mysterious. The summer she'd turned fifteen—that was when she'd first seen him, walking along the beach. She'd been too shy to approach him. She'd just stood and watched how his dark hair lifted in the breeze, and how golden-brown his shoulders looked in the sun. He had seemed so unattainable, a boy you only dreamed about. But then he had come back to town the next summer, too, the summer Lisa turned sixteen.

She went to check on the spaghetti sauce. It ought to simmer a bit longer; she supposed she could finish the salad. She scattered fresh mushroom slices over the lettuce, but then she ran out of inspiration. Once again, she looked into the living room. Amy had knelt down beside their mother's chair, and was talking earnestly to Helene. Their voices were low, and Lisa couldn't catch what they were saying, but the conversation seemed too intense to be simply about lime or cherry soda. Couldn't Amy let up a little? No matter how much she wanted it, she couldn't force Mom and Dad to get back together.

Lisa's gaze flickered to the opposite side of the room. Patrick lounged on the sofa, regaling Jon with stories of the flight from Connecticut. Lisa could all too plainly catch *his* voice.

"Lisa's certain it must have been the airplane food," Patrick said. "But I told her that airplane food never disagrees with me. I'm used to traveling everywhere." He gave a self-deprecating laugh. "Everywhere but Florida, I suppose."

Patrick looked pleasingly handsome as he sprawled on the sofa, his fair complexion perfectly complemented by his white cotton shirt. White was his best color, something he seemed to know well. It made him appear so clean. Lisa had never realized that before. Patrick always looked as if he had just stepped out of the shower. And he always smelled fresh, as if he had just patted shaving lotion on his cheeks. Why did that suddenly make Lisa grimace?

Jon sat on the other side of the sofa, listening to Patrick with an air of resigned patience. Then his gaze drifted toward Amy, and Lisa saw the unmistakable love in his eyes. She felt like a voyeur, witnessing a moment not meant to include her.

Swiftly she went to the opposite side of the counter so that her back was to the living room. She began slicing carrots for the salad, trying to concentrate on this one, simple task. Instead, she almost cut her finger with the knife. What was wrong with her? Why couldn't she just accept seeing Jon and Amy together? It wasn't that she begrudged their love. It wasn't that she still wanted Jon for herself. Whatever had existed between the two of them had died a long time ago. Maybe, if she were honest, what disturbed her most was that Jon and Amy were so right for each other. They were so happy, and it was the kind of happiness you couldn't help envying. It seemed something special, unique, the kind of emotion you believed in only when you were very young. Sixteen, perhaps...

"I told Amy I'd help with lunch. She's treating me with kid gloves, but I am *perfectly* capable of handling spaghetti."

Lisa was startled by the sound of her mother's voice behind her.

"Mom...hi," she said lamely. She and Helene had already exchanged rather awkward greetings today, but nothing they'd said had dispelled the long-standing tensions between them. Lisa had never experienced outright arguments or differences of opinion with her mother. No, it was something more subtle than that, an inability to go below the surface with each other. Even as a child, Lisa had checked any extremes of emotion around her mother, knowing instinctively to restrain herself.

Perhaps she'd simply wanted to please Helene. After all, Helene herself had always been so calm and gracious. Lisa had tried to emulate her, perfecting her role as the quiet, obedient daughter. But then she'd turned sixteen, and done something no obedient daughter ever should. She'd gone too far with Matt Connell—so far that a frightening new world had opened before her. If only she could have confided in her mother about it! But the training of her childhood had been too strong. Lisa had gone on pretending to be the quiet one, the one who didn't cause any trouble. No one had known her fear. Not her mother, not her father, not her sisters. Lisa had been alone in the midst of her own family, but that had seemed far better than risking the loss of her family's love. Back then, she couldn't imagine any of them loving her if they ever learned the truth.

She was an adult now, not the vulnerable kid she'd once been. What had happened to her at sixteen was something long buried—no need to bring it up after all this time. Nonetheless, the careful politeness she and her mother had observed for years was starting to show the strain. It manifested itself in uncomfortable pauses, sentences left dangling. Lisa wondered what would happen if she ever did try to have a real conversation with her mother. Not about Lisa's own personal life, of course—that would be just a little *too* real. But there were plenty of other topics that might take them below the surface. Would Helene be horrified at the possibility? Did she ever talk about emotions with anyone? Or was the problem simply one between her and Lisa, the youngest of her daughters? Lisa had grown so distant from *all* the family that she couldn't answer any of these questions.

Helene went to the stove and stirred the sauce. "Imagine," she said. "Amy makes this from scratch. She stews the tomatoes, everything. It would be much more convenient just to open a bottle."

Lisa almost had to smile at that. Amy's recipe for homemade spaghetti sauce had been handed down from Helene herself. All during the time Lisa and her two sisters had been growing up, Helene had taken pride in providing the family with home-cooked meals. Now, however, Helene took pride in tossing frozen dinners into the microwave. It seemed to be one of the many small rebellions she'd embarked upon lately.

Helene took another pot, filled it with water and placed it on the stove. She cranked the heat on high. "I told Amy you and I would finish up in here. She needs to spend more time with Jon."

Lisa glanced into the living room yet again. Jon and Amy now sat together snugly at one end of the sofa, chatting with Patrick. Correction: Jon and Amy were gazing into each other's eyes while Patrick chatted.

"Your Patrick seems to be a very nice man," Helene said. Those were exactly the words Amy had used—"your Patrick." And the phrase was still annoying. Lisa reminded herself how lucky she was to have Patrick.

"He *is* very nice," she said. She tried to ignore

what a bland word that was. "Nice." It was the type of word people used when they couldn't think of anything else to say about someone. It was a word that they hid behind.

Lisa elaborated. "He's not just nice. It's more than that. He's...considerate. After all, he didn't really have to come on this trip with me. It took some rearranging of his schedule to do it. Which means he's supportive. And responsible."

"I'm glad for you, dear. He sounds like a fine person, exactly the kind of man you deserve." Helene uttered these statements in a formal manner, as if congratulating an acquaintance. Her expression carefully portrayed nothing more than benign interest. Lisa experienced a spark of irritation that surprised her with its intensity. Again she wondered what it would be like to have a real conversation with her mother.

Maybe it was time to find out.

CHAPTER TWO

THE GROUNDS APPEARED as fussy as ever to Matt Connell. Clipped lawns, dressed gardens, manicured shrubs—the place looked as if it had just got the full treatment at the local beauty parlor. A fence cut its way along the perimeter—a whimsical half-moon fence, pickets a dazzling white. At the center of this fussbudgetry stood a house like a chamber of commerce postcard—the abode of Matt's grandmother, one Bea Connell.

Ignoring the pain in his knees, lower back and right shoulder, Matt walked up the bright brick pathway to his grandmother's front door, wondering, not for the first time today, what the hell he was doing here. Sure, he had received a telegram from the old gal, imploring him to "forgo his self-imposed exile long enough to help her put her affairs in order." Grandma Connell, it seemed, was preparing to call it quits at the tender age of eighty-one—not an entirely unsympathetic situation, unless you considered that she had been threatening such a demise as regularly as clockwork for the last decade and a half.

Bea, Bea, busy as a bee. Growing up, Matt had spent many a summer here along the gulf helping

"Busy-as-a-bee Connell" tend her ostentatious grounds. Looking back reluctantly, Matt supposed he had not been the easiest of teenagers to raise, and it had, no doubt, been a respite for his parents to ship him off to Florida for the hot months of summer. To Matt, they had been months from hell, toiling away under the callused green thumb of Grandma Connell.

Then, however, Matt had discovered the girls of Hurricane Beach. And one of the girls he'd discovered had been Lisa Hardaway.

As a teenager, Lisa had been pretty but tentative. She'd seemed uncertain about everything she did, as if waiting for someone to give her permission to enjoy herself. Yet there'd been nothing tentative about her in the drugstore this morning. She'd been cool and very much in control. Her vague prettiness had deepened into genuine beauty. She reminded him of a pale, irresolute sketch that had gained contour and color over the years, resulting in a vivid portrait. The new confidence in her eyes made them seem a darker brown. Her hair had turned from flaxen to gold, her girl's body had become a woman's.

Matt felt a stirring of some long-ago emotion, but he kept it at a distance. His summers in Hurricane Beach belonged to another life. Lisa Hardaway belonged to another life. The stirring of emotion inside him flickered, then died, just as it should.

Ignoring his grandmother's doorbell, Matt

rapped twice on the brass knocker—an elaborate affair depicting two lovers kissing.

"Bea," he called. "Bea, it's me." Without waiting for a response, he opened the door, which was never kept locked, and stepped inside. The house was as hot as ever…stiflingly hot. For some reason, Grandma Connell preferred to take her fresh air only out in her gardens. In her house, windows were never opened, air conditioners never switched on, and over the long Florida summers the place built up heat like a furnace, baking the furniture and people inside.

"Bea…it's only Matt. No need to relinquish your deathbed just to answer the door."

He walked across the living room and down a short hall. By the time he reached the kitchen, he already had beads of perspiration on his forehead, and he could feel his shirt begin to liquify.

"Lord, it's hot in here," he grumbled as he headed straight for the refrigerator, popped open the door and leaned his head and shoulders inside.

"Mathias T. Connell. You'll foul the ricotta!"

Matt turned his head enough to observe Grandma Connell striding into the kitchen. For a woman threatening death, she had the gait of an Olympic distance walker. "It's good to see you, too, Bea," he said. "Oh, and by the way, you're welcome."

Despite her trademark scowl, Grandma Connell almost gave Matt a little smile. "Butterscotch?"

He held the bag of candy out to her.

"Now, Matt," she said as she snatched the bag

from his hand, "you shouldn't have. You know I won't eat them. They'll just go stale in the cupboard."

Matt didn't bother answering this. Grandma Connell's penchant for butterscotch was almost legendary. "So," he said, opening the freezer compartment and fishing out a handful of ice. "What's got into you this time, Bea? All this talk about putting your affairs in order... Did old lady Waverly's roses outshine yours again? Or did Mr. Potts neglect to be first on your dance card?"

Busy-as-a-bee Connell had already busied a butterscotch out of its wrapper and into her mouth.

"Mathias, don't be rude. Janet Waverly is over three years younger than me. If she's an 'old lady,' then I'm a dinosaur."

Matt put the ice on the back of his neck and closed the refrigerator. "Tyrannosaurus...Tyrannosaurus Connell. Except you're too stubborn to be extinct."

Grandma Connell did smile this time, although Matt thought there was something vacant in her usually bright eyes.

"You are okay, aren't you, Bea?"

"Mathias. My sweet Mathias." Grandma Connell moved to the counter and dumped her butterscotch candy into a tulip-shaped dish. The sly old gal had had a bowl out and waiting. "You know, Matt, your Grandpa Mathias was always so very proud. 'Such a fine namesake,' he was fond of saying. 'Such a fine boy.'"

"You must be joking," Matt said. "Grandpa

Connell hardly ever said two words to me besides
telling me what a slacker I was down at the found-
ry. 'Pick up your feet, Matt. I never saw anyone
move so slow in my life. Are you sure you're alive
in there, Matt? Pick up your feet.'''

Grandma Connell turned to give him a stern
look. ''That was just his way, Matt. Being hard on
the ones he loved most was just his way. First your
father...and then you. He loved you both dearly.''

At the mention of his father, Matt felt a stillness
inside. It was dangerous, for into the stillness the
memories could come. If he started thinking about
his father, then he'd think about the rest of them,
too. He couldn't allow that.

He did what he always did at such times—with
a force of will, he took himself from the past and
centered himself firmly in the present. He didn't
look back, he didn't look forward. He was here in
his grandmother's house, that was all.

Despite the ice at the back of his neck, despite
having just extracted himself from the fridge, Matt
was sweating profusely now. Grandma Connell's
skin, on the other hand, was as dry as sunbaked
leather—except for around her eyes. Matt thought
he detected some beads of moisture around Bea
Connell's eyes.

''What's happened, Bea?'' Matt stepped closer
and placed his non-iced hand on his grandmother's
shoulder. ''Everything is all right, isn't it?''

But the only answer Matt received was a hug—
a frail and tender hug from his grandma Connell.

LISA WATCHED as Helene dumped the pasta into the pot of boiling water. Helene didn't speak, just hummed a little under her breath. Lisa realized that was a sound she'd heard often while growing up— her mother's quiet humming. It had seemed comforting, something you could count on, like the whisper of the wind or the lapping of waves against the shore. Now Lisa wondered if her mother's humming wasn't just a way to avoid uncomfortable conversations.

Lisa began slicing mushrooms. "You know, Mom," she said in a casual tone, "it isn't very often that all of us have a chance to get together."

"I realize that, believe me," Helene said, looking genuinely wistful. "I've wished so many times to have all three of you here. You and Amy and Meg."

"Meg will be flying in next week," Lisa reminded her. "You'll have your wish."

"Not really. It would be so much better if all three of you could live nearby. We could be a family again."

"I guess that's what we all want," Lisa said. "To be a family again." She hoped that she sounded sincere. Truth was, she'd spent the last decade trying to get as far away from her family as possible. *That,* however, was not germane to the discussion.

"I think about it a lot," Helene murmured, absentmindedly stirring the spaghetti. "How the three of you came along when I'd just about given up hope. You were my lovely, unexpected gifts. First one happy surprise, then later another...and another. I couldn't get over how lucky I was. Not just one beautiful little girl, but three, as if to make up for all the years without.''

Lisa had heard these words often; they were part of the Hardaway lore, as familiar as the bedtime stories Helene had once read to her three young children. But usually Helene said, ''You were *our* gifts,'' making clear that both she and Dad had been delighted with such an unexpected bounty of daughters. Today, however, any reference to Merrick Hardaway seemed pointedly left out.

Lisa scattered the sliced mushrooms on top of the lettuce. ''Mom,'' she said. ''You know what I meant. We can't be a family again without him. Without Dad.'' There. She'd actually broached the subject. No more pretending that her father had simply disappeared.

''I think we could use some olives in that salad, don't you?'' Helene said, completely ignoring Lisa's remark. She poked her head in the refrigerator. ''I saw a jar of olives in here the other day. Yes...here we are. Why don't you slice a few of them, dear? It's a nice touch, olives in a salad.''

Lisa tried again. ''Mom,'' she said. ''If you'd just talk about it, maybe it would help.''

Helene paused. ''There's nothing to talk about,'' she said. ''Except for the fact that we're all starving, I'm sure.'' She checked the spaghetti sauce. ''Mmm...almost done. Why don't you taste it?'' She smiled too brightly.

Helene had lost none of her soft beauty over the

years. Her skin, despite the fine wrinkles, had a pretty rose color. Lisa remembered so well being a child, climbing into her mother's lap and touching her face. Helene had always been one for hugging and kissing her children. If the words had never come easily between her and Lisa, there had always been the hugs and kisses.

Lisa remembered other things, such as the way her mother had always seemed to be listening for something no one else could hear. She would hold her head ever so slightly cocked, as if expecting some private summons. Then Merrick would call out to her from another room in the house, and that seemed to be what she'd been waiting for.

Lisa tried slicing a few of the olives, but they kept skittering away from her on the cutting board. She set down her knife with a clatter. "Mom, it's just not right. I know *he* wants to be with you. I mean, this whole argument has gotten out of hand! If the property is causing you so much trouble— just sell it. Get rid of it. Then maybe you and Dad could…I don't know, travel together. See a few of the sights you've always talked about." Even as she spoke, Lisa realized how hollow the words sounded. And now Helene gazed at her almost with haughtiness.

"Lisa," she said, "do you truly believe this is only about whether or not we're going to sell the property? Is that what you think?"

The question took Lisa by surprise, for she'd expected another evasion. And she really didn't know *what* to think. Last spring, Amy was the one who'd

called her in Connecticut and informed her that
their parents were in the midst of a marital crisis.
Over the next few months, the crux of the matter
had emerged: a land developer from Atlanta by the
name of Palmer Boyce wanted to buy the Hardaways' extensive beachfront property, including the
home where Helene and Merrick had raised their
three daughters. The two senior Hardaways
couldn't seem to reach a joint decision on the matter.

Admittedly, Lisa had speculated whether or not
this disagreement was the only trouble between her
parents. But Helene and Merrick had always
seemed so devoted to each other—and they'd been
married almost fifty years, after all. What else
could be the trouble?

"I'm a good listener," Lisa said now, purposely
keeping her tone nonchalant. "That's what I've
been told, anyway. Maybe you could give me a
try."

For a moment she sensed a wavering in her
mother, and was certain she even saw a flash of
pain in Helene's eyes. But then Helene resolutely
shook her head. "I told you. There's nothing to talk
about. Now, what else do you think we can do with
this salad? I'm positive we can liven it up a bit."

Lisa saw the moment slipping from her, but she
didn't know how to reach her mother. There was
something new about Helene these days, a certain
implacability that showed itself now and then. Always Lisa remembered her mother's softness—but
there was no evidence of it today.

Lisa gazed at the salad, wondering what could be more enlivening than mushrooms and olives. She also wondered why she couldn't seem to talk to anyone in her family. Talking—and listening—to people in trouble had become her specialty. Her master's in psychology gave her the credentials she needed, but it was also something intuitive with her, knowing when to prod a reluctant teenager into speech, or when to let silence do its work. She was even adept at mediating between kids and their frantic parents. Why, then, couldn't she talk to a single person in her own family?

"Sure smells good in here," said Patrick as he strolled into the kitchen. "I'm actually starting to feel hungry again."

"I knew you'd be better in no time," Helene said, clearly relieved at the intrusion. "With all this lovely sunshine, no one can feel bad for long. Well, let me go tell Amy and Jon we're almost ready. We'll have a delightful lunch together." Murmuring these superficial remarks, Helene hurried from the kitchen.

Lisa stared after her in frustration. She felt a completely immature urge to yank at her mother's skirts and demand that she come back here. But then Patrick distracted her, wrapping his arms around her from behind and giving her a squeeze.

"I really do feel better," he said. "Whatever you got me this morning did the trick."

Lisa felt engulfed. She slipped away from him and pulled open the refrigerator door. "Mom says the salad needs spicing up, but I don't see anything in here that'll help."

"Nuts," Patrick said.

She glanced over her shoulder at him. "What's wrong now—"

"Put nuts on the salad," he said with a grin. "Cashews, walnuts, whatever. That always does the trick."

Lisa found herself gritting her teeth again. Patrick had a habit of saying that something or other "did the trick." It had never bothered her until now, and she supposed she was just on edge. It had not been a restful day so far.

She rummaged through a cabinet and found some pecans. "I don't really think so," she began.

"Sure." Patrick took the nuts from her, and sprinkled a generous amount on the salad. "Didn't I tell you I worked as a chef's helper once? I was only fifteen, but I was out there slaving away in a restaurant six nights a week."

Lisa had heard about every one of Patrick's jobs as a boy. He could justifiably gloat over the fact that he'd worked his way all through high school and college, and then gone on to establish his own business. He now had three safe and lock shops in Connecticut, with plans to open a fourth. If he wanted to explain for the hundredth time how he'd been a chef's assistant, or a bag boy, or a hardware clerk, or how he'd once juggled two paper routes— certainly he had a right.

He went to stir the spaghetti sauce, tasting a little

from the spoon, and Lisa told herself that she'd better learn how to relax her clenched jaw.

"Your sister's a good cook," he said. "Too bad you didn't pick up a few tricks from her."

"Amy has all kinds of talents," she said. "Maybe you'll find out you picked the wrong sister—except that Amy is most definitely taken."

Patrick instantly looked penitent. He came over to Lisa and put his arm around her. "Sweetheart, I was only kidding," he said. "I like doing all the cooking. You have more important things to do."

Patrick was simultaneously demonstrating several of his best qualities: he was a man who didn't mind taking over in the kitchen; he respected Lisa's immersion in her career; and he never complained about the many hours she put into it. He was also very, very perceptive.

"You know," he said, "you've been acting funny ever since this morning. Like something's bothering you."

Patrick's arm felt heavy around her shoulders, but she forced herself to stay motionless. "I warned you this trip wouldn't be pleasant," she said. "My family and I—let's just say we don't know what to do with each other."

Patrick gave her a shrewd glance. "Nah...it's more than that. You've been acting strange ever since you got back to the bed-and-breakfast this morning. You resent the fact that I got sick, and made you run errands."

"Don't be silly," Lisa said. "You weren't even sick. You just had a touch of indigestion, and—"

"My point exactly. You figured I was making too big a deal about my stomach."

Was it Lisa's imagination, or had she discerned just a bit of self-righteous innocence in Patrick's voice? One way or another, she was never going to hear the end of his confounded stomach problems.

"Look," she said. "I know you didn't feel well. And I was more than happy to go out and get you something. I'm glad you're doing better." She slipped away from him once more and studied the salad. If only she could get rid of all those pecans.

Patrick leaned against the counter, practically taking it over. "Something else is bothering you," he said. "Fess up."

There he went again—dissecting her emotions. "It's nothing," she muttered.

"What happened this morning?" he persisted.

"Don't be ridiculous—"

Patrick had that look on his face, the one that said he was on the trail of discovery. This was when he became his most persistent—when he was probing Lisa's emotions. If he sensed that anything in the least was troubling her, he seemed to consider it his duty to get it out in the open and resolve it. If he made her life miserable in the process, well, he seemed to consider *that* an unfortunate side effect.

"This is how I see it," Patrick said. "This morning we were relaxing at the B&B, having a good time. Except for my stomach, of course. Then you went out to get me something at the drugstore.

Ever since you got back, you've been…different. Tense. Wound-up.''

"Patrick, would you give it a rest? I just don't like being in this town.''

"Here. I'll show you.'' He put his arm around her shoulders again. "Aha,'' he said with satisfaction. "Look at that—the minute I touch you, there it is. You stiffen right up. And, if I'm not mistaken, in the next few seconds you'll find an excuse to pull away from me.''

It took quite some effort for Lisa *not* to pull away. She reminded herself that this was one of the main qualities that had drawn her to Patrick in the first place: his sensitivity to her emotional needs. How many men could claim the same talent?

"You're making too big a deal out of this,'' she said.

Patrick appeared thoughtful. "If it was only the town that bothered you, you would've been acting strange since the plane landed yesterday. But you weren't. It only started this morning—''

"For crying out loud!'' Too late, Lisa realized she'd raised her voice. The occupants of the living room—Amy, Jon, Helene—all turned their heads to glance curiously toward the kitchen. Lisa took a deep breath, and when she spoke next her voice was almost a whisper. "You know what your problem is, Patrick? You don't understand how to take a vacation. When you're not working, you just don't have enough to occupy your mind.''

"You know there's something you want to tell me," he whispered back in a conspiratorial manner. "You send out these little signals, and it's up to me to interpret them. For some reason, you can't seem to tell me straight out how you feel. You want me to take the responsibility for worming it out of you. It's an assertiveness problem."

That did it. Lisa pulled away, then turned to confront him. "I ran into someone at the drugstore, all right? A...friend. From a long time ago. It got me to thinking about a few things. It's that simple, that ordinary." Only the last part was a lie. Nothing about her memories of Matt Connell was simple or ordinary.

"Male or female?" asked Patrick.

"What are you talking about—"

"This friend of yours," he said with exaggerated patience. "Man or woman?"

"Man," she said tightly.

Patrick grinned. "Ah...so now we're at the bottom of it. You, Lisa, ran into an old boyfriend. And it's bugging you no end."